ABBY AND TESS

PET

D0826643

Rabbits Don't Do Homework

BOOK 8

written by
TRINA WIEBE

illustrated by
MEREDITH JOHNSON

Lobster Press ™

To all the wonderful kids and teachers at Kelly Creek Community School. – Trina Wiebe

Rabbits Don't Do Homework
Text © 2009 Trina Wiebe
Illustrations © 2009 Meredith Johnson

Published in 2009 by Lobster Press™
1620 Sherbrooke Street West, Suites C & D
Montréal, Québec   H3H 1C9
Tel. (514) 904-1100 • Fax (514) 904-1101 • www.lobsterpress.com

Publisher: Alison Fripp
Editor: Meghan Nolan
Editorial Assistants: Mahak Jain & Nicole Watts
Graphic Design & Production: Tammy Desnoyers
Production Assistant: Leslie Mechanic

We acknowledge the financial support of the Government of Canada through the Book Publishing Industry Development Program (BPIDP) for our publishing activities.

 We acknowledge the support of the Canada Council for the Arts for our publishing program.

The Canada Council | Le Conseil des Arts
for the Arts | du Canada

Library and Archives Canada Cataloguing in Publication

Wiebe, Trina, 1970-
    Rabbits don't do homework / Trina Wiebe ; illustrator, Meredith Johnson.

(Abby and Tess, pet-sitters, 1499-9412 ; 8)
ISBN 978-1-897550-01-4

    1. Rabbits–Juvenile fiction. I. Johnson, Meredith. II. Title.
III. Series: Wiebe, Trina, 1970- . Abby and Tess, pet-sitters ; 8.

PS8595.I358R32 2009   jC813'.6   C2008-904651-X

Printed and bound in Canada.

Text is printed on Rolland Enviro 100 Book, 100% recycled post-consumer fibre.

TABLE OF CONTENTS

CHAPTER 1

A Canine Client?

"Pssssst!"

Abby looked up from her notes.

"Pssssst! Abby ... turn around!"

Abby glanced at Mr. Laurent, her sixth-grade teacher, who was writing on the board at the front of the class. Quickly, she turned in her seat and grabbed the paper that Dinah held toward her. Abby unfolded the note and hid it in her lap.

"We have a job for you. Meet us after school. From, D and D."

Abby grinned. A job! It had been months and months since her last pet-sitting job working with an African gray parrot named Chiko. She'd taken Chiko into the hospital where her dad worked, to help cheer up a patient. Chiko was great, but it hadn't been like her usual pet-sitting jobs where she got to feed and care for the animals herself.

That was the whole reason why she had started her pet-sitting business, after all. If she was going to be a veterinarian when she grew up, she needed all the experience she could get. The apartment building her family lived in had a strict "NO PETS ALLOWED" policy, so Abby, along with her little sister Tess, took care of other people's pets. She had hoped to pet-sit dogs. Any kind of dogs. Big dogs, little dogs, it didn't matter to her. Dogs were her absolute favorite animals in the whole world.

Since then, she'd taken care of a lot of animals ... everything from ants and fish to hamsters and goats. But not a single dog. Could this be her big break? Could she finally be pet-sitting a canine?

Quickly, she scribbled on the bottom of Dinah's note. *What kind of animal?*

Abby crumpled the note into a tiny ball, too excited to re-fold it. She turned in her seat and gave Dinah the thumbs up sign. Then she dropped the note and kicked it under Dinah's desk with her foot.

But Dinah didn't pick up the note. Instead, her cheeks grew pink and she hunched over her desk and began writing furiously.

Mr. Laurent cleared his throat. He sounded close. Too close. With a sinking feeling, Abby turned and found him standing beside her desk.

"Abby, you're not passing notes again, are you?"

Abby's face felt hot. "I'm sorry," she stammered.

He bent down and picked up the crumpled paper. "I believe you dropped this," he said, handing it to her. "You know where the trash can is, don't you?"

"Yes, Mr. Laurent," mumbled Abby. She felt the whole class staring at her as she dropped the note into the trash and hurried back to her desk. Dirk and his best friend, Zack, snickered as she passed them. Dinah smiled apologetically as Abby sank into her chair.

Now she'd have to wait until school was over to find out what kind of animal it was. A whole hour, according to the clock above the classroom door. Abby stifled a sigh. Grade six was totally different from grade five. Abby was a good student and liked learning new stuff, but even she thought Mr. Laurent was a little homework-crazy. Grade six was serious business.

Mr. Laurent clapped his hands. "Okay, class. I know everybody is looking forward to spring break."

Dirk and Zack mouthed "Yes!" and gave each other a high-five.

Mr. Laurent frowned and continued. "However, I do expect you to complete the assigned math questions, study the spelling list, finish the French worksheets, and one last thing ... I want a two thousand-word essay on how you spent your holiday. You will read these essays to the class when we return to school."

Groans filled the classroom. Only Abby's hand shot up in the air.

"Can I write about dogs?" she asked.

Mr. Laurent shook his head. "Not this time, Abby."

"What if I spend my holiday taking care of a dog," she persisted, thinking about Dinah's note. "Can I write about that?"

"No dogs, Abby," he repeated. "Everything you've done this year has been about dogs. Stories about heroic dogs. Reports about unusual dogs. You've written dog poems and painted dog portraits in art class. I think it's time to branch out."

"But ... " Abby began.

Mr. Laurent crossed his arms over his chest. "No more dogs."

Abby slumped down into her seat. *Fine*, she thought. She wouldn't write the essay about dogs. But that didn't mean she wouldn't spend her entire spring break – maybe, just maybe – taking care of her very first doggy client!

CHAPTER 2

Babies Don't Make Good Pets

Finally, the bell rang.

"Whoot, whoot!" shouted Dirk, jumping out of his seat so fast his desk nearly tipped over. The class erupted into a flurry of action as chairs scraped across the floor and kids chattered excitedly as they stuffed their books into their backpacks. Abby expected Mr. Laurent to hush them, but he looked almost as happy as the class.

"Meet us by the flagpole," Dinah called to Abby as she pushed her way out of the classroom.

Moments later, Abby headed toward the grassy patch where the flagpole stood. To be honest, she had been kind of dreading spring break. Things were crazy at home. But the thought of a pet-sitting job changed everything, so she ran the last few steps. Dinah, and her identical twin sister Dana, were waiting for her.

"How are the babies?" asked Dana before Abby could bring up the job.

"The babies?" Abby dumped her backpack on the ground. "They're okay, I guess."

"Can we come see them today?" asked Dana. "Please? We haven't seen Seth and Ian since they – "

"Were born," continued Dinah, jumping into the middle of her sister's sentence. "They're just the cutest little things! You're so lucky to have baby brothers. Twins, just like us!"

"Yeah, lucky," Abby mumbled.

At first Abby had been super-excited about Mom's pregnancy, just like everybody else. She'd been looking forward to playing with the baby and feeding it and cuddling it. She'd thought it would be kind of like having a new puppy. Two new puppies, as it turned out. Not!

The first thing Abby learned was that babies cried. A lot. They cried when they were wet, when they were hungry, when they were tired ... and with twins it was like they were crying in surround sound.

The second thing Abby learned was that babies pooped. A lot. They pooped before a feeding, after a feeding, and even during their naps. The apartment was filled with diapers – folded stacks of clean diapers and buckets of stinky dirty diapers. Abby had scooped plenty of pet poop during her pet-sitting jobs, but it was nothing compared to this.

Also, it turned out that babies weren't so good at playing. Their necks were wobbly and their skulls were soft and they had zero attention span. Not that Abby could get near them most of the time. Mom and Dad hovered over them constantly. Even her little sister Tess, who usually made a career out of being Abby's shadow, was completely obsessed with the babies. Their tiny apartment was jam-packed with people, and yet Abby felt invisible sometimes.

After a whole month of this, just hearing the word "babies" was enough to make Abby want to scream.

"So can we see the babies?" asked Dinah and Dana together.

Abby forced a smile on her lips. "Sorry, Seth has a runny nose and Mom is paranoid about germs."

"Darn," said Dana, disappointed. "Oh well, maybe after spring break. We're visiting our grand-parents for the whole week. Which reminds me, we have a – "

"Job for you," finished Dinah. "Our auntie is going out of town for a few days and needs someone to look after her pets."

Abby perked up. "Pets? Plural? As in more

than one?"

Dinah nodded.

"Puppies?" Abby dared to ask, crossing her fingers behind her back. *Please, please, please,* she thought.

The twins hesitated.

"Well..." said Dana.

"They're soft and furry, just like puppies," said Dinah.

"And they're smart and friendly," added Dana. "Just like puppies."

"And they like to chew on things," said Dinah. "Just like puppies."

Abby couldn't stand it any longer. "If they're not puppies, then what are they?" she demanded.

Dinah and Dana exchanged glances. "Easter bunnies!"

CHAPTER 3

Abby Meets the Easter Bunny

Abby frowned. "Easter bunnies? Is this a joke?"

"It's no joke," Dinah assured her. "Auntie Jo has two pet rabbits. Binky and Marbles. She got them from the Rabbit Rescue Center where she works. And they really are Easter bunnies. Some kid was given them for Easter last year, but he got tired of taking care of them. It happens a lot."

Abby was intrigued. She'd never looked after rabbits before! "When can I meet them?"

"How about now," said Dana. "Since Seth has the sniffles."

"Great!" Abby grabbed her backpack. "Let's go."

"Um, aren't you forgetting something?" asked Dinah.

Abby stared at her blankly.

"About this tall," said Dana, holding her hand at shoulder level. "Freckles, pig-tails, answers to the name Fido. And Rover. And sometimes Spot."

Abby closed her eyes for a moment. She'd been so excited about the new job that she'd nearly forgotten about Tess. Not only was Tess a partner in their pet-sitting business, but they had to walk home from school together every day. It was one of Mom's rules.

With a sigh, Abby took a deep breath and put two fingers in her mouth. She let out a wolf-whistle so loud it echoed off the merry-go-round and bounced off the monkey bars.

A moment passed.

"Should we look for her?" asked Dana.

Abby shook her head. "Just wait."

Another moment passed, and then they heard barking. The barking grew louder as Tess raced up, ran circles around them, then plopped down on her haunches and panted happily.

Abby sighed. Her parents assured her that acting like a dog was just a phase, one Tess would outgrow when she was ready. Abby was certainly ready. The constant barking, drooling, and growling got on her nerves.

"Knock it off," she said as Tess pawed her leg eagerly. "We've got a pet-sitting job."

Tess barked. "Yippee!"

The four girls walked down the street. The fresh smell of cut grass filled the air and Abby found herself looking forward to this new job. She'd earn a bit of money, which was always nice, but the best thing would be getting to spend time with a couple of cute bunny rabbits. And it would be the perfect excuse to get out of the apartment, away from all the baby craziness!

Maybe spring break wouldn't be so bad after all.

Abby laughed and chatted with Dinah and Dana as they walked. Even Tess, racing ahead to sniff at mailboxes, couldn't dampen Abby's good mood.

"We're here," announced Dinah.

Abby glanced up at the house, then stared, her mouth hanging open. It was *the* house. The house of her dreams. The one she imagined when she thought of her family finally moving out of their cramped, smelly apartment. It was exactly the way she'd pictured it ... a pretty blue house with white shutters and trees and flowers and a yard just the right size for a puppy. A dormer window tucked into the attic seemed to wink down at her, as if the house recognized her, too.

"Are you okay?" asked Tess, tilting her head

quizzically.

"Uh, yeah," stammered Abby. "Sure."

Dinah unlatched the gate. "Well, don't just stand there ... come on! Auntie Jo should be home from work by now."

Abby and Tess followed the twins up to the front door. Abby didn't see a rabbit hutch anywhere. *Maybe it's in the backyard*, she thought. She watched while Dinah rang the doorbell, then opened the door and stuck her head inside.

"Auntie Jo? We're here!"

Abby heard a muffled reply from somewhere in the house. They stepped inside and found themselves in a sunny sitting room.

"Make yourselves comfortable, girls," called a voice from upstairs. "I'll be right down."

Abby and the twins sat on a plump sofa while Tess sniffed a hard rubber teething ring. Other toys lay scattered across the floor, and a green ball sat beside the sofa. Tess nudged the ball with her nose, and it rolled away, jingling as tiny bells tumbled around inside of it.

"Don't touch anything," hissed Abby.

Tess ignored her and disappeared through an open doorway.

"Does your Aunt have kids?" Abby whispered to Dinah. She had noticed the house was baby-proofed, just like their apartment. Houseplants, which Abby knew could sometimes be poisonous, were up high, out of reach. The electrical outlets had covers to keep out tiny fingers. Even the television and lamp cords were covered in hard plastic tubing.

"Nope," grinned Dinah. "Just rabbits."

Abby was puzzled. "But don't rabbits live outside? You know, like my Gran's farm animals?"

Before Dinah could answer, Tess burst back into the room, her eyes wide with surprise. Behind her came a furry brown ball with its ears hanging low, brushing the floor with each hop. Tess leapt into Abby's lap as a second furry ball, this one white, hopped into the room.

The brown rabbit grunted a warning. It thumped its powerful back leg on the floor twice, then froze, staring at them.

Tess yelped.

Startled, the white rabbit darted under the sofa, leaving behind a few brown droppings the size of chocolate-covered peanuts.

Abby stared at the rabbit poo, then met Tess's eye. What exactly were they getting themselves into?

CHAPTER 4
Homework for the Holidays

Auntie Jo came down the stairs and laughed. "I see you've met Binky and Marbles!"

The brown rabbit hopped across the floor and tugged at the hem of her jeans with its teeth. Auntie Jo bent down and petted the rabbit's head. It ground its teeth gently and closed its eyes in contentment. Auntie Jo gave it one last rub behind the ears, then she stood and walked over to the girls.

She was a tall woman, older than Abby had expected. Almost as old as Gran, probably. Her hair, which was curly and kind of wild, was streaked with grey. She wore a shirt with the words "Rabbit Rescue" stitched across one sleeve.

"I'm Josephine Peebles, but please call me Jo. Dinah tells me you are qualified pet-sitters, which is wonderful, because I'm going on a trip next week. Are you available?"

Tess yipped as Abby pushed her off her lap and jumped to her feet to shake Auntie Jo's hand.

"Of course!"

Auntie Jo smiled. "Wonderful. Have you looked after rabbits before?"

"No," Abby admitted. "But we've looked after lots of different kinds of pets, and we're very responsible. Right, Tess?"

Tess eyed the brown rabbit warily. "I guess."

Abby flushed. What kind of answer was that? "We've got plenty of references," she assured Auntie Jo.

Just don't call Dirk, from class, thought Abby. They'd pet-sat his ant colony one time and had nearly destroyed it. And maybe not Mr. Maggioli, whose lizard, Angus, had escaped for a little while. And definitely not Mrs. Wilson, whose goldfish had accidentally gotten a bubble bath.

"That won't be necessary," said Auntie Jo. "Dinah tells me you're the right person for the job."

Abby breathed a silent sigh of relief. Maybe those other pet-sitting jobs hadn't gone perfectly, but in the end, the pets were safe and Abby had learned a lot about caring for animals. This new job should be a piece of cake.

"I have a few questions," Abby said in a business-like voice. She ticked them off on her fingers. "What kind of rabbits are they? What do they eat, and how much and when? Do they get vitamin supplements? Where do they sleep? How much exercise do they need? Should I ..."

Auntie Jo laughed and held up her hands. "Goodness! Dinah said you were serious about your job, and she was right."

Abby unzipped her backpack and pulled out some paper. She liked to keep notes, especially on new jobs. The more she knew about the animals, the better she could take care of them. Tess sidled up to her and put her mouth to Abby's ear.

"When can we go home?" she whispered. "I want to see the babies."

Abby frowned. This was Tess's pet-sitting job too. She used to love being with Abby and spending time with the animals. Of course, that was before the babies were born. All of a sudden she had turned into a guard dog, hovering over them protectively. In the grocery store she bared her teeth and growled when people came too close to the twins. It was embarrassing.

"Shhh," Abby whispered back. "You're being rude."

"We can go over this another time," offered Auntie Jo. "My trip isn't until next week, and I'm sure your mother is expecting you home soon."

It was true, Abby realized. Mom *would* be wondering where they were. That was another thing that changed when the babies were born. Abby still had the key to the apartment on a string around her neck, but she didn't need it anymore. Mom was home every day after school now, instead of working at the college, where she taught art classes. Abby had thought this would be one change she'd really love, but even though Mom was home, it seemed as if she was too busy with the babies to do anything fun.

"I want to see the babies," whined Tess.

"Fine." Abby stuffed the paper back into her bag. "I guess I can do some research online."

"Extra homework? On spring break?" said Dana. "You must be crazy."

"Animal crazy," said Dinah. "That's why she's such a good pet-sitter."

"You know," said Auntie Jo, walking with them to the front door, "if you're really interested in learning more about rabbits, you could come down to the Rabbit Rescue Center with me. We're always looking for volunteers."

"Really?" Abby was interested in anything that

gave her a chance to be around animals. Plus, helping at the rabbit Rescue Center would be the perfect thing to write about for Mr. Laurent's essay. There wouldn't be a dog in sight!

"Of course," Auntie Jo said. For a moment she looked troubled. "We take in as many rabbits as we can, but it costs an awful lot of money to run the shelter. Without our volunteers, I don't think we could keep the shelter running."

"Poor bunnies," said Dinah. Dana nodded.

Tess whined and scratched lightly at the front door.

"Talk to your parents," said Auntie Jo. "If they give their permission, then why don't you meet me here tomorrow morning, around ten. I'll take you to the shelter and introduce you to everybody."

"I'll be here," promised Abby. It was the perfect chance to spend time with animals *and* make a real difference in the world. This might just turn out to be the best spring break ever!

Chapter 5
The Great Wall of Diapers

"We're home," shouted Abby. She was so excited about volunteering at the Rescue Center that she could hardly stand it. She shrugged out of her backpack, kicked off her shoes, and skipped down the hallway.

"Woof, woof!" barked Tess. She raced past Abby, anxious to see the babies.

Mom stepped out of the nursery, which used to be her art studio and really should have been Abby's new bedroom. She held up her hands. "Shhh! I just got the twins to sleep!"

Tess's shoulders slumped. "Aw ... I haven't seen them all day."

Abby was glad the twins were asleep. Now she could talk to Mom without any interruptions. "Guess what? I've got the best news ever – "

An unhappy wail interrupted her, almost immediately joined by a second wailing voice. Tess yipped with delight and dashed into the nursery.

Mom sighed and gave Abby a quick half-hug. "Hold that thought, honey. Seth's been so fussy today – I think he has gas – and Ian seems to cry just to keep his brother company."

Abby sighed and watched Mom disappear into the nursery. Sure, she understood that babies were a lot of work, and having two meant double trouble, but these days life was just an endless round of feedings, burpings, and diapers.

As if on cue, Mom called, "Abby? Could you grab me some more diapers? They're in your bedroom."

"My bedroom?" Abby didn't like the sound of that. She walked into the room she'd shared with Tess for years and stopped dead in her tracks. It was a small bedroom, with barely enough room for two twin beds and a dresser. The messy half was Tess's and the tidy half was Abby's. It was almost as if an imaginary line had been drawn down the middle of the room.

But now that line wasn't so imaginary anymore. A wall of cardboard boxes was stacked nearly to the ceiling in the space between the two beds, dividing the room in half. There were enough diapers here for an entire year. Maybe two!

She opened a box marked "extra small" and

carried a package of disposable diapers back to the nursery. Seth lay on the soft changing pad, gurgling and enjoying being diaper-free.

Abby handed Mom a clean diaper and quickly stepped away, out of the danger zone. She'd already learned to be careful around babies with their diapers off. Like the underground sprinkler system at the park, they could go off at any time.

Mom held out the dirty diaper, wrapped into a tight ball. Grimacing, Abby pinched it between two fingers and dumped it into the garbage in the corner.

"Pe-yoo," whimpered Tess, covering her nose.

"Mom, can we talk?" Abby asked. She'd rather discuss the pet-sitting job and the Rescue Center when she had Mom's full attention, but that didn't look likely to happen any time soon.

Quick as a flash, Mom had Seth wrapped, snapped, and dressed again. She glanced at Abby with an apologetic smile. "I know what you're going to say. But there was a great diaper sale at the bulk store and I didn't have anywhere else to put them. I know, I know," she added, when Abby opened her mouth. "I wasn't going to use disposable diapers. They're just terrible for the environment. But honestly, Abby, right now I need all the help I can get."

Abby felt a twinge of guilt. She knew she hadn't been much help lately. "That's okay, Mom," she said. "It's kind of like having my own room now."

Mom laughed weakly. "Yeah, kind of."

Abby decided to talk to Mom at supper, when Dad would be home too. "Why don't you go lie down," she suggested. "Tess and I can watch the babies until Dad gets home."

Mom hesitated. "Are you sure?"

Abby nodded and picked up Ian, careful to support his neck. His hair stood up in spiky little tufts and he smelled like baby shampoo. "We'll play some music. You know how much the twins love that singing monkey."

Mom carried Seth and Abby carried Ian into the living room, where two sets of infant swings stood side by side. Carefully, they buckled the twins into the swings, and gently set them in motion.

"Maybe I'll rest my eyes," Mom said, sinking into the couch. "Just for a few minutes ..."

Abby smiled as she realized that Mom was already asleep. Tess dashed into the kitchen for a snack and for the first time in days, Abby had her brothers to herself.

Seth gurgled. Ian sucked on his fingers and

gazed at her with his clear blue eyes. Abby couldn't help but smile. *They really are cute,* she thought.

"Maybe I haven't given you guys a fair chance," Abby whispered to them. "I'll try to spend more time with you. You'd like that, wouldn't you?"

Ian belched and smelly white spit-up oozed down the front of his shirt. The swings slowed down and Seth squinched up his face.

Simultaneously, the twins began to howl.

CHAPTER 6

Caught!

Ian was cranky, so Dad played with him the moment he got home from work. Seth was fussy, so Mom made supper while she carried him in his baby sling, like a baby kangaroo. And after dinner both Ian and Seth were tired and grouchy so Abby cleared the table while her parents and Tess took them for a walk in their double stroller.

It was nearly bedtime and Abby still hadn't been able to tell her parents about the new pet-sitting job, or get permission to volunteer at the Rescue Center in the morning.

"Well, at least it's quiet," she said out loud.

She decided to do some research. The more she knew about rabbits, the better prepared she would be to take excellent care of Binky and Marbles. This was one job where nothing was going to go wrong.

She pushed Tess's disgusting old chewy bone off the chair and sat down in front of the computer. It was squeezed into a corner of the living room,

mostly because there was no other place in the apartment to put it, but also because Mom and Dad liked to keep an eye on it.

Abby knew all about online safety. She knew that she was never to give out personal information or share her password or download anything without asking first. She also knew she really wasn't supposed to go online without her parents' permission. Unfortunately, they were busy with the babies right now.

As usual.

And this was research, after all. Abby stared at the keyboard. Where to start? She typed the word "rabbit" into the search engine that Dad always used. In the blink of an eye, a page full of rabbit links popped onto the monitor.

"Over seventy-one million results?" she said, dismayed.

She started clicking. She learned that rabbits were small mammals in the family *Leporidae*. People kept them as pets, but they were also raised for meat and their fur was used for clothing. They were the fourth sign of the Chinese zodiac.

None of this helped Abby one bit.

Then she noticed links to several Rabbit Rescue organizations. She clicked on the first one and read about the people who saved abandoned rabbits. She found pictures of Holland Lops, which looked just like Binky and Marbles, with their ears hanging down on either side of their heads. She was so engrossed in her research that she didn't realize her family was home until she felt Dad's hand on her shoulder.

"What are you doing, Abby?"

Abby almost jumped out of her skin. "Dad!"

He looked at the computer. "I thought we had an agreement. No parents, no computer."

"This is research," she said quickly. "It's like homework."

Dad raised one eyebrow. "You still should have asked."

Abby knew he was right. She crossed her arms and stared at the carpet. "It's just that I was so excited about Binky and Marbles and volunteering, but you and Mom were too busy to hear about it, and Tess cares more about the babies than our pet-sitting business and..." She broke off, annoyed by the tears that welled up in her eyes.

"Whoa," said Dad. "Okay, start at the beginning."

So Abby did. When she was done, Dad smiled, but his eyes looked tired. "I guess things have been a bit crazy around here since the twins were born," he said.

Abby nodded.

"It won't be like this forever," he assured her. "Babies grow quickly. Things will get back to normal as they get bigger – "

"Bigger?" Abby cried. "There's barely enough room for them now!"

She and her dad looked around. The furniture was jammed together to make space for the baby swings, the bouncy chairs, the stroller ... not to mention the baskets of toys and books piled on the coffee table. When Abby had tried to take a shower last night, she'd found the tub full of washed and folded baby laundry.

"My bedroom is full of diapers," said Abby in a small voice.

Abby and Dad stared at each other, then burst into laughter. Dad pulled Abby into a bear hug until her giggles turned into hiccups.

"Okay, here's the deal," Dad said. "I'll give Mrs. Peebles a call. I think volunteering at the Rescue Center is a wonderful way to spend your spring break. I know Mom will be proud of you too. But from now on, you must follow the computer rules. No exceptions, not even for research. Understand?"

Abby nodded. "I promise."

"Good." Dad glanced up at the sound of crying. "Must be bath time. I'd better go help. And you'd better get ready for bed because you've got a big day ahead of you."

Abby grinned. Just thinking about all the rabbits she would be helping gave her a tingle of excitement. She couldn't wait. Tomorrow would be her first day as a real live volunteer!

CHAPTER 7

To the Bunnymobile!

"Wake up, Tess," Abby whispered.

Tess growled, then rolled over. The blankets bunched up over her head, exposing her feet. Her pillow lay on the floor and there were toys and dirty socks mixed in with the bedding.

"Come on," insisted Abby, shaking Tess gently. "Get up, partner."

"I don't want to," came Tess's muffled reply.

Abby hesitated. Usually Tess was the one waking Abby up in the mornings, pawing at her covers and snuffling in her ear. Suddenly, things were reversed.

"This is your last chance," Abby threatened. "Get up or I'll go without you."

Tess poked her head out of the covers. "I want to stay with the babies. We're taking them for their checkup today."

Abby sighed. The last time they had taken the twins for a checkup, Tess went into full-blown guard dog mode. She didn't budge an inch from the twins, protecting them from the other children in the waiting room, and glaring at the nurse who weighed and measured them.

"Besides," Tess added. "You're not pet-sitting. You're just going to that rabbit place."

"Fine," said Abby. She knew she should be happy that for once, she got to do something interesting without Tess tagging along. So why did she feel disappointed? She shrugged and ran outside where Dad was waiting in the car.

Just before ten o'clock Dad pulled up in front of Auntie Jo's house.

"Nice place," he commented. "It reminds me of the house I grew up in." Then he leaned over and kissed Abby on the nose. "Have a good time today."

Abby jumped out of the car and raced up the front path. She couldn't wait to see the rabbits again. She rang the doorbell and waved as Dad drove away.

Auntie Jo opened the door. "Right on time!"

Abby peeked inside. "Where are Binky and Marbles? In the backyard?"

"Heavens, no," said Auntie Jo. "Binky and Marbles are house rabbits. It wouldn't be safe for them to be outside alone. They have an enclosed run for fresh air and exercise, but only when I'm around to supervise."

"They live in the house with you all the time?" asked Abby. She thought for a moment. "What about ... you know ... when they have to ... go?"

"How do you think Marbles got his name?" laughed Auntie Jo. "Don't worry, I'll explain everything before I go on my trip. Right now we need to hop into the Bunnymobile."

Abby raised one eyebrow. "Bunnymobile?"

"My mini-van," admitted Auntie Jo. "The Center can't afford it's own vehicle, so we use mine. You can fit a lot of rabbits in a mini-van."

When they arrived at the Rabbit Rescue Center Abby was a little disappointed. The building wasn't much to look at ... just a drab square building squeezed between a hardware store and an office supply shop.

"I know it doesn't look all that special from the outside," said Auntie Jo, catching the expression on Abby's face. "But just wait."

A bell tinkled overhead as Auntie Jo pushed open the glass door. Abby found herself in a small waiting room, just like at the doctor's office – except the furniture was a little more worn, and a little more out of date. The floor was scuffed and the walls needed a coat of paint, but the receptionist was friendly.

"Hi, Jo. Who's your friend?" she asked.

Auntie Jo gently pulled Abby forward. "This is Abby. She has a knack with animals, so I thought we could put her to work around here."

"Do you think I'll get to rescue some rabbits today?" asked Abby.

"You make us sound like superheroes," the receptionist said with a laugh. "Mostly volunteers help with rabbit care. You know, cleaning cages, bunny socializing, that kind of thing."

"Bunny socializing?" repeated Abby.

Auntie Jo nodded. "That's just a fancy term for spending time with the rabbits. Petting them, talking to them, helping them become comfortable with humans. Some of these poor animals have been badly neglected."

"Go on in," said the receptionist. The phone rang and she turned to answer it, waving Auntie Jo and Abby toward a door behind her desk.

Abby followed Auntie Jo into the back room. She couldn't believe she was going to spend the whole morning playing with animals. Did rabbits like being scratched behind the ears like like puppies did? Would they let her pick them up and pet them? Would they bite her?

She was about to find out!

CHAPTER 8
Superheroes Come in All Shapes and Sizes

The back room was filled with wire cages. Many of the rabbits appeared to be sleeping, but a few looked up as Abby approached.

"Wow." Abby had never seen so many rabbits in one place before.

"Rabbit over-population is a problem," Auntie Jo explained. "Rabbits can begin breeding at about six months old. They kindle, or give birth, about 31 days after mating, having five to ten kits, or babies, each time. Multiply that over several years, and factor in all those babies having their own babies ... well, you get the idea."

Abby gulped. Even without a calculator, she could tell that was a lot of rabbits. "Where did they all come from?" she asked.

"Different places," said Auntie Jo. "Sometimes owners bring them to us when they realize they can't care for them anymore. Sometimes we learn about cases of abuse and we have to go and rescue the rabbits. Many of them come from larger animal shelters. If they can't find a home for the rabbits, we bring them here so they don't have to be euthanized. Do you understand what that means?"

Abby nodded. She knew that sometimes a vet will give an animal an injection that makes them fall asleep and then stop breathing. It was the kindest way to end a hurt or sick animal's life.

"Here we care for our rabbits until we find homes for them," Auntie Jo explained. "Our volunteers even provide foster homes when our center gets full."

Abby's heart ached for these gentle animals. "I wish I could be a foster parent too." She thought of their apartment. Even if there was room, which there wasn't, the building was still strictly "NO PETS ALLOWED."

"Volunteering your time is a tremendous help," said Auntie Jo. "Come, I want to introduce you to someone."

She led Abby to a cage that held a small brown rabbit. "Abby, meet Cocoa Bean. She's new here, and I think she could use a friend. Often, rabbits come in bonded pairs, but this little one is all alone."

Abby leaned close. Cocoa Bean flattened herself against the floor of the cage.

"It's okay," said Abby softly. "I won't hurt you."

"You have good instincts," Auntie Jo told her.

"Rabbits don't like loud noises or sudden movements. They are prey animals, you know. In the wild they have to be ready to flee from danger. So it's important to be gentle with them and gain their trust."

Abby and Cocoa Bean gazed at each other. Cocoa Bean took one hop toward Abby, then another. She stared at Abby, her nose twitching.

"Oh, Crystal," Auntie Jo called, waving at one of the volunteers. "Could I borrow you for a moment?"

A girl much older than Abby walked over. She was dressed in black, wore a lot of make-up, and had a streak of purple in her long dark hair.

"Crystal is one of our junior volunteers," said Auntie Jo. "You can ask her any questions you might have while I go take care of some office work."

With that, Auntie Jo disappeared back into the reception area, leaving Abby and Crystal looking at each other.

"Hey," said Crystal.

"Uh, hi," said Abby.

Crystal jerked her chin toward the rabbit cage. "So, you want to hold Cocoa Bean?"

"Yes, please."

Crystal opened the wire door and reached inside for Cocoa Bean. She rubbed the rabbit behind

the ears and then gently scooped it up. Holding it firmly against her chest, she cooed in its ear.

"Why don't you go over there," Crystal said to Abby, indicating an area with several cushions and toys scattered about. "It's safer if you sit on the floor."

Abby sat cross-legged on a pillow and Crystal put Cocoa Bean in her lap. The brown rabbit squirmed a bit, then settled down. She was warm, and Abby could feel her heart beating beneath her silky fur.

Abby hesitated. "What am I supposed to do?"

Crystal rolled her eyes. "Just talk to her or whatever. Let her play with a toy if she wants. Anything is better than being locked up in a cage all day, don't you think?"

"Um, yeah," Abby agreed. She put her hand on Cocoa Bean's head, aware of Crystal's sharp gaze.

"You look like a real live chocolate Easter bunny," Abby told Cocoa Bean. The small rabbit twitched its ears. "I wish I could take you home with me."

"I can't believe you just said that," snapped Crystal. She crossed her arms and glared at Abby. "That's the whole problem now, isn't it?"

Abby gulped. She'd only been a volunteer for a few minutes, and she was already in trouble. But what had she done wrong?

CHAPTER 9

Bunny Hop

Abby looked at her. "I don't understand."

"People give bunnies as gifts, especially at this time of year. They're so adorable ... who can resist? But loads of those bunnies end up right here, with us." Crystal snorted and shoved some clean hay into Cocoa Bean's cage. "Or worse, stuck in a box in the backyard day and night, alone and forgotten. It's so unfair!"

"I wouldn't do that," said Abby.

Crystal stopped what she was doing. She looked at Abby, then sighed. "I'm sorry. I'm not mad at you. It's just that I get so frustrated sometimes."

"That's okay," Abby said. "It's really sad seeing all these rabbits in here."

"These are the lucky ones," said Crystal. She finished cleaning and filling Cocoa Bean's food dishes and came and sat beside Abby. "Some people let their rabbits loose, thinking they will be just fine in the wild. Except, of course, the rabbits don't have a clue how to survive."

"Oh," said Abby.

"Someday I'm going to fight for animal rights and stop animal cruelty," Crystal said, her eyes bright with passion. "I'm going to be a lawyer or an animal advocate or run an animal shelter like this one. You just wait and see."

Abby believed her. "I'm going to be a vet."

"You'll help lots of animals then, too," Crystal said. She grinned and pointed at Cocoa Bean. "Hey, look, she's chinning you."

Abby glanced down. Cocoa Bean rubbed her velvety chin on Abby's arm, again and again. She twitched her nose, then hopped off Abby's lap to investigate a chew toy.

"Chinning means she likes you," explained Crystal. "Rabbits have scent glands under their chin, and they rub their scent on things that belong to them."

"Scent glands," repeated Abby. "Just like a cat, right?"

"Yup," agreed Crystal. "Cocoa Bean's a pretty happy bunny. Sometimes she even dances. You've heard of the bunny hop, right?"

Abby glanced at Crystal to see if she was being serious. "Bunny hop?"

"Watch."

Crystal rolled a soccer ball towards Cocoa Bean. It stopped near the rabbit's nose. Cocoa Bean sniffed it, then hopped in a circle around it. She nudged the ball, then hopped in another circle. Suddenly she jumped in the air, twisting her body and flicking her ears joyfully.

Abby giggled. "She does dance!"

"It's called a 'binky'," said Crystal. "It's a rabbit happy-dance."

Aha, thought Abby. *Now I know how Auntie Jo's other rabbit got its name, too!*

They played with Cocoa Bean, watching her push the soccer ball back and forth across the floor, until Auntie Jo poked her head in the room.

"Abby? You ready to go?"

Abby wasn't really, but she nodded. "I'll just put Cocoa Bean in her cage."

"Be gentle," advised Crystal. "Put one hand under her ribs, and scoop up her bum with your other hand. Hold her close to your chest so she feels safe."

Carefully, Abby picked up Cocoa Bean and carried her back to her cage. She gave the rabbit an extra pat on the head and then made sure the door was latched securely.

"I'll come back and see you again," she promised. Cocoa Bean blinked, then hopped to one corner and burrowed in the clean hay.

Just before Abby and Auntie Jo headed out the door, Crystal rushed up to them. "These are for you," she said, shoving a handful of pamphlets into Abby's hands. "Everything you need to know about taking care of house rabbits. You know, since you're going to be a vet and all." Crystal turned and stomped back into the center, but not before Abby caught a glimpse of a smile on her face.

"I think you made a friend," Auntie Jo said as they drove away in the Bunnymobile. "Crystal doesn't warm up to just everyone, you know."

"I think I made two friends," Abby replied with a smile, thinking of Cocoa Bean. She wondered if Binky and Marbles would bunny hop too. Or chin her or play pass with a soccer ball.

She couldn't wait to try her brand-new bunny socializing skills on them next week!

CHAPTER 10
Separation Anxiety

Abby volunteered every day at the Rabbit Rescue Center. She helped Crystal clean cages and replace the food and water before they sat together and socialized with one or two of the rabbits. She felt a bit guilty about leaving Mom at home with Tess and the babies, but the rabbits really needed her.

Soon it was the day before Auntie Jo's trip.

Abby dressed quickly, then found Tess in the nursery, winding the musical mobile that hung over Seth's crib. Tess hadn't come to the Rabbit Rescue Center even once, but today was different. Today was official pet-sitting business.

"Auntie Jo is giving me instructions for taking care of Binky and Marbles today," she told Tess. "Are you coming?"

Tess tickled Seth's toes and giggled when he kicked his chubby legs in the air. She looked at Abby. "Can the babies come too?"

"Of course not," said Abby. "They're too little."

"But I'll miss them," wailed Tess. "Can't we bring them in the stroller? I'll take good care of them."

"We're being paid to take care of the rabbits, not the twins," Abby reminded her.

Tess was quiet. "Can I at least bring a picture of the babies?" she asked finally.

Abby let her breath out in a soft whoosh. For a moment, she'd thought Tess was going to quit the pet-sitting business altogether. It wasn't that Abby couldn't handle things without her. In fact, sometimes things went a little haywire when Tess was on the job. But they'd started this business together, and they were a team. At least they had been, before the twins were born.

"Sure," Abby said, trying not to sound too relieved.

It took them less than ten minutes to walk to Auntie Jo's house. Abby rang the bell.

"Good morning, girls," Auntie Jo greeted them. "Please ignore the mess, I'm in the middle of packing."

"Where are you going?" asked Tess.

Abby nudged her in the ribs. "Don't be nosy."

Auntie Jo laughed. "That's okay. The truth is, I'm thinking of going back to university."

Tess scratched behind her ear. "Aren't you too old to go to school?"

Abby wanted to put her hand over Tess's mouth, but the words were already out. Luckily, Auntie Jo just laughed.

"You're never too old to learn something new," she said. "I'm a bit tired of rattling around in this empty house all by myself. It's time for a new adventure."

"I think it's a great idea," Abby said quickly, before Tess could say anything else. She glanced around wistfully. "Although I'd sure love to live in a house like this. It's so nice."

"It is a lovely house for a family," agreed Auntie Jo. "But it's a bit big for just one person."

"I'll bet it would fit six people perfectly," Abby said under her breath. It was so easy to imagine her family living here.

"Things a bit crowded at home?" asked Auntie Jo.

Abby blushed. She hadn't meant for Auntie Jo to hear her. "Well, you know, with the twins and all ..."

"Oh, I understand," Auntie Jo assured her. She led them into the kitchen. "I'm sure Crystal has already taught you quite a bit about caring for rabbits," she began. "So let me just show you where everything is. Beginning with food – "

"Fresh pellets, hay, veggies, and water every day," Abby ticked off on her fingers. "The food and water dishes need to be washed daily and any uneaten food is put in the compost."

At the word compost, Tess wrinkled her nose. "Yuck."

Auntie Jo smiled at Abby. "Crystal has taught you well. Okay, next ... their cage."

"I thought they were house rabbits. Why do they need a cage?" asked Abby. She looked around. "Where are they, by the way?"

Tess sniffed the air suspiciously, first in one direction, then the other. "Yeah, where are they?"

"In the playroom," said Auntie Jo. "That's where I keep their cage. Even rabbits who have the run of the house like to have a safe place to nest in."

They walked down a short hallway. "This used to be my guest room, but now it's the bunny playroom."

Abby looked around curiously. This room, like the rest of the house, was completely bunny-proofed. The electrical outlets had safety covers and there wasn't a cord or wire in sight. Brightly colored cat and parrot toys lay scattered on the floor. She counted at

least a dozen toilet paper tubes and an old phonebook lying on the floor. The pages had been gnawed, as though someone had been snacking on them but got full somewhere around the letter "G".

"Wow," Abby said, impressed.

Tess snorted. "The babies have better toys."

"Look, Tess," Abby said, pointing at several boxes with windows and doorways cut into them. Some of the boxes were joined together, making tunnels. It looked like a cardboard castle. "We used to do that when we were little, remember?"

A furry brown face poked through a cardboard window and stared up at Abby. A furry white face poked through another window.

Abby giggled. "Hi, guys."

"The rabbits play hide and seek and chase in these boxes all day long," Auntie Jo told her. "And when they get tired of that, they chew on the walls."

Abby knew rabbits loved to chew. Their teeth never stopped growing, so it was important for them to always have safe things to chew on. Bunny teeth were sharp!

"You'll need to give them fresh hay for bedding," Auntie Jo instructed. "And of course, you'll need to clean out the..."

Just then Tess let out a howl. Instantly, the rabbits disappeared into their cardboard hiding places. Yowling, Tess raced away from the cage she had been investigating. She grabbed Abby around the stomach, burying her nose in Abby's shirt.

"I see you've found the litter box," said Auntie Jo.

CHAPTER 11
Reduce, Reuse, and Rabbit Recycle

"Rabbit poo," yelped Tess. "Gross!"

"What did you expect?" laughed Abby. If Tess had come to the Rabbit Rescue Center, she'd know that rabbits are pretty easy to litter train.

"The clean litter is here," said Auntie Jo. She opened a cabinet, showing Abby several large bags. "It's made from recycled newspaper, which is good because the rabbits tend to nibble on it. Regular kitty litter can make them very sick."

"Did you hear that, Tess?" asked Abby. "Rabbits are good for the environment."

"Rabbits are extremely eco-friendly," Auntie Jo agreed. "In fact, you can put the used litter and the rabbit droppings straight into the compost."

Abby wasn't convinced. "Even the poo?"

"Absolutely." Auntie Jo said. "Rabbit droppings contain nitrogen and phosphorus, which are excellent for the garden. "

"Recycled poo?" Tess pinched her nose. "Yuck."

"Don't try it with cats or dogs though," warned Auntie Jo. "Manure from a meat-eating animal can transmit parasites or disease. Also, don't be alarmed if you notice the rabbits eating their droppings. They actually have two kinds of poo, round firm ones that go in the compost, and soft squishy ones called cecotropes, which they eat. The cecotropes have good bacteria in them, to help with their digestion."

Tess looked a little green.

"It's actually very healthy," Auntie Jo assured her. "Sort of like a cow, chewing its cud."

"Oh." Abby felt a little queasy herself.

"Carry the litter box outside and dump the whole thing in the compost. Then rinse it with vinegar water," Auntie Jo said, pointing at a squirt bottle filled with a clear liquid. "And you're done. Of course, you might find a few stray droppings here and there. Just pick them up with a tissue."

"No way, Jose," cried Tess. "I'm not picking up rabbit poo!"

"What's the big deal?" asked Abby. "You watch Mom change a hundred diapers a day."

"The twins don't poop on the floor," argued Tess.

"Well, diapers aren't exactly eco-friendly," Abby shot back.

"Taking care of the food and litter box shouldn't take more than a few minutes," said Auntie Jo, interrupting the argument. "However, I'd like you to spend some time each day socializing with Binky and Marbles. They're a bonded pair, so they do a wonderful job of keeping each other company, but they still can get bored now and then. And bored bunnies get into mischief."

Abby was pretty much an expert on bunny socialization by now. "No problem." She paused. Auntie Jo had mentioned the word "bonded" before. "What does bonded mean?"

"Bonding is an amazing life-long friendship ... bonded rabbits groom each other, keep each other company, even nurse each other through illnesses," Auntie Jo explained. "It's not good to separate bonded rabbits. If one is sick, they both go to the vet."

"Like me and the twins," cried Tess. "We must be bonded too!"

Abby didn't say anything. Tess *did* have a strong relationship with the twins, something very special. Something Abby was maybe missing out on.

"Now," said Auntie Jo. "Why don't you girls get to know Binky and Marbles while I go make some lemonade?"

Auntie Jo left and Abby knelt by the cardboard castle. Almost immediately, a furry brown nose peeked around the corner. Abby smiled. Binky hesitated, then hopped toward her, nudging her leg with his nose.

"Hi, Binky," Abby said gently. "Wanna play?"

Tess came over. "Rabbits can't play."

"Sure they can," said Abby.

"Really?" Tess looked down at Binky, then crossed her eyes and waggled her tongue.

Binky blinked.

Tess turned around in a circle, plopped on the floor and scratched behind one ear, her tongue hanging out the side of her mouth.

Binky hopped away, alarmed.

"The twins always laugh at that," complained Tess.

"Try throwing him a toy," suggested Abby. "Maybe he'll play catch."

Tess rolled her eyes. "You're teasing me."

Abby picked up a colorful teething ring. The twins had one exactly like it. "No joke, Tess. Toss this to Binky."

Tess shrugged and flipped the teething ring through the air. It landed on the floor in front of

Binky. Binky's nose twitched, then he hopped forward and nuzzled the toy.

"The twins can do better than that," scoffed Tess. "And they can't even walk yet."

"Watch," advised Abby.

Binky pushed the teething ring this way and that way with his nose, then he opened his mouth and nibbled on the hard plastic. Quick as a wink, he picked it up in his teeth and flung it in the air.

Tess gasped.

Abby laughed. "Cool, huh? The rabbits at the center like to throw things too."

"Again!" crowed Tess.

Abby tossed the teething ring to Binky, who

tossed the toy in the air.

Sometimes Binky would throw the ring, hop after it, and throw it again. Sometimes he sat on it and Abby had to nudge him aside. Once he tossed the ring right into Tess's lap. Pretty soon Abby and Tess were breathless from laughing.

"Binky is pretty neat," admitted Tess. She rubbed his soft fur.

"Okay, girls, please come wash your hands," said Auntie Jo from the doorway. "We'll have some lemonade and you can tell me all about those new baby brothers of yours."

"I've got a picture of them," Tess told her, scrambling to her feet. She dug through her pockets. "They're so cute... hey, the photo's gone!"

Instantly, Marbles and Binky disappeared into their cardboard castle.

"Don't shout," warned Abby. "Rabbits don't like loud noises."

"But it was right here," Tess cried. "Where did it go?"

"It probably fell out when we were playing with Binky," Abby said, scanning the floor.

"Oh dear," said Auntie Jo. "Marbles can be mischievous. She may have taken the photo to her nest."

"Marbles," groaned Abby. "We were so busy playing with Binky, we weren't watching Marbles."

Tess hurried to the cage. Frantically, she pawed through the hay, using both hands to scoop it between her legs and into the air behind her. Soon she pulled out the photo. It was wrinkled and bent and one corner was nibbled off.

"Marbles kidnapped the twins!" wailed Tess.

CHAPTER 12
Bunny Babysitting

"Hurry up, Tess!" Abby pounded on the bathroom door. It was the next morning and she was anxious to start pet-sitting. "Binky and Marbles are waiting!"

Her answer was the sound of the toilet flushing.

Abby sighed. Tess was obviously still upset. She had refused to even look at Marbles after the photo incident yesterday.

"C'mon," Abby said through the door. "The rabbits will be getting hungry."

She heard the taps run. Then stop. Then run again.

"The faster we leave," she said, "the faster we'll be done and you can get back home to the twins."

The door opened a crack. "Will we be back before they're finished their nap?"

"Maybe," Abby said, glancing at her watch.

Tess stepped into the hall. She wore the "Proud Big Sister" T-shirt that Mom and Dad had given her. It had a picture of the twins on the front, inside a big heart. Abby had the same T-shirt, but it was still in her dresser drawer.

"Fine," said Tess. "Let's go."

"Great." Abby grabbed her hand and dragged her toward the apartment door. "Let's get out of here before Mom – "

"Abby?" called Mom from the nursery.

Too late.

"Could you please write yams on the grocery list for me? Gran can't come for Easter dinner this year, but I thought I'd cook up a nice meal anyway."

"Okay," Abby called back.

"Oh, and could you add pecans too? I might make a pie."

Abby sighed. "Sure."

"Have you seen Seth's musical mouse?" Mom poked her head out of the nursery. "He's a bit fussy today."

It took them a whole five minutes to find the musical stuffed toy, wedged behind the seat of Seth's infant swing. Growling, Tess wrestled it out of the swing and carried it to the nursery in her mouth. She dropped it at Mom's feet, smiling expectantly. Abby suspected that if she'd had a tail, it would be wagging. Finally they were out the door and on their way.

"I miss the babies," said Tess with a sad sigh.

She patted Seth and Ian's faces on her shirt and glanced at Abby. "Don't you?"

Abby laughed. "We've only been gone a few seconds."

"What if they start crying and Mom needs me to make my funny faces?" asked Tess. "What if they can't fall asleep without me singing them a song?"

"Mom can handle it," Abby assured her.

"But what if – "

"The babies are fine, for goodness' sake!" Abby snapped. "They probably won't even notice we're gone. Binky and Marbles, on the other hand, are depending on us."

"Don't you like the babies?" asked Tess in a small voice.

Abby stared at Tess. What a foolish question! "Of course I like the babies."

Tess frowned. "I think you like all those silly rabbits better."

"What?" cried Abby.

Tess shrugged. "You spend all your time at that rabbit place."

"They need me," Abby tried to explain. "And the babies have you and Mom and Dad. Plus it's crowded in the apartment and the babies cry all the time, and the rabbits are quiet, and well ..." her voice trailed off. Why did her reasons sound like excuses?

Tess looked down at the sidewalk and they walked the rest of the way in silence. Abby found the key to the front door under the doormat, just as Auntie Jo had promised. She unlocked the door and they let themselves in.

Tess headed for the playroom and Abby headed for the kitchen. On the fridge was a printed list of veggie do's and don'ts. Under the "do" heading, there was a long list of things like bok choy and beet greens and carrots. Beside it, Auntie Jo had scribbled, "Pick three!" The "don't" list was much shorter. It had things like rhubarb and beans on it. Beside that, Auntie Jo had written, "Toxic!!!"

Abby pulled open the fridge and found it full of plastic containers. She chose one at random and opened it. Carrots. She picked another that turned out to be sliced green pepper, and a third that was leafy parsley.

"Tess," she called. "Can you bring me the food dishes?"

There was no answer from the bunny playroom.

"Tess?" Abby tried again.

Still no reply.

Sighing, Abby left the vegetables on the counter and headed down the hall. She pushed open the playroom door, then smiled when she saw Tess sitting in the middle of the floor, cuddling with both rabbits. It looked as if she'd forgiven Marbles for yesterday's photo disaster.

Tess looked up. "Aren't they cute?"

"Yup," Abby agreed. "And I'll bet they're hungry too. Why don't you fill their food dishes while I take care of the litter box?"

"Okay," said Tess. Gently, she nudged the rabbits off her lap and got to her feet. "I think they really like me. They hopped right into my lap, and we've been playing the whole time, and ... what? Why are you staring at me like that?"

Abby bit her lip. Oh no! The rabbits were hungrier than she thought!

"I didn't sit in poo, did I?" cried Tess, checking her pants.

Abby shook her head. "Tess, why don't you come to the kitchen with me," she began.

Tess brushed at her T-shirt. "What? Do I have hay on me?"

"No, it's not that..."

Tess's hand froze. Slowly, she looked down at her T-shirt. There, right where Seth's cute little baby nose used to be, was a frayed, rabbit-gnawed hole.

CHAPTER 13

Let's Make a Deal

"Don't panic," Abby said quickly. "We can fix it."

Tess took deep gulps of air. "Seth's nose is ... is ... gone!"

"It's okay," Abby reassured her. She glanced down and saw Marbles now nibbling on Tess's shoelace. Gently, she nudged the rabbit aside with her foot and led Tess out of the playroom. "Everything will be fine, I promise."

"His nose!" Tess's voice rose in a wail. She threw back her head and howled mournfully. "She chewed off his nose!"

"Shhhh," Abby warned. She pulled Tess into the kitchen. "You'll upset the rabbits."

Tess's face flushed a bright pink. "I'll upset *them*?"

"Marbles didn't mean any harm," Abby said quickly. She needed to soothe her sister, before she had a total meltdown. "Maybe we can sew it. Or

Mom and Dad can order a new shirt."

Tess poked her finger through the jagged hole. It looked like she was picking Seth's nose. She glared at Abby with wild eyes. "First the photo, now this. These rabbits are so mean!"

"You can't blame the rabbits," Abby argued. "They were just doing what comes naturally. You can't take it so personally."

"They didn't chew your special baby shirt," Tess pointed out. She wiped away a tear with the back of her arm. "How come you never wear it? I bet you'd wear it if it had Binky and Marbles on the front."

"What are you talking about?" Abby demanded.

"I think you like the rabbits more than the babies," Tess said flatly.

Abby groaned. "Not this again."

"It's true." Tess's voice wavered. "I'd rather be with the babies. And you'd rather be with the rabbits."

Abby didn't like where this was leading. "Tess, be reasonable ..."

"Maybe I should just quit," Tess said.

For a few moments, the kitchen was quiet. Was this the end of "Abby and Tess, Pet-Sitters"? If they dissolved the partnership, Tess could spend all her

time at home playing with the twins and Abby could spend all her free time at the shelter and pet-sitting. That's what they both wanted, wasn't it? Everyone would be happy.

Except Abby knew she wouldn't be happy at all.

It seemed as if her whole life had turned upside down the day that the twins were born. Everything had changed ... her parents didn't have time for her and it felt as if there wasn't any room for her in the apartment anymore. She didn't want her business to change too. She would miss pet-sitting with Tess.

"Do you really want to quit?" she asked Tess.

Tess wiped her nose on her sleeve and sighed. "No."

"Let's make a deal," Abby proposed. "You give pet-sitting the rabbits another chance, and I'll ..." She wracked her brain. What could she use to bargain with? "I'll give you my 'Proud Big Sister' shirt. It'll be a little big, but you'll grow into it."

Tess shook her head.

Abby tried to think fast. "I'll buy you a new chewy bone. Or a new flea collar. Or take you for walks in the park more often."

"Nope," said Tess.

"Well, what do you want?" asked Abby.

"What will make you stay?"

Soft footsteps thumped down the hallway toward the kitchen. Abby and Tess looked up as Binky and Marbles hopped into the kitchen, noses twitching. Binky stopped in front of the fridge, and Marbles bumped into him. Playfully, they hopped around, bumping and nuzzling each other.

"They sure love each other," Tess said, watching them snuggle affectionately. Marbles licked Binky's ear.

"Friends for life," Abby agreed. "It's that special bond Auntie Jo was talking about."

"That's what I want," Tess decided.

"I'm not grooming you, if that's what you're thinking," Abby warned.

"No," said Tess. "I want some of that bonding stuff."

Abby tried to keep the impatience out of her voice. "What are you talking about?"

"Bonding," Tess said. "I'll try harder with the pet-sitting, if you try harder with the babies."

"That's ridiculous," Abby sputtered. "I don't need to bond with the babies. We like each other just fine."

Tess crossed her arms over her chest. Seth and Ian peeked out at Abby too. Abby looked from the three of them to the rabbits on the floor, which were now giving each other bunny kisses.

"Whatever," Abby finally said. It was crazy, but then again, everything was crazy these days. "You win, Tess. I'll spend more time with the babies."

CHAPTER 14
Monkeying Around

Tess was true to her word. The next day she gave the rabbits celery and kale and fresh drinking water without complaint. Only once did Abby catch her gnawing on a carrot meant for the rabbits. She even held the door open while Abby dumped the litter box into the compost bin in the backyard.

"Let's take Binky and Marbles outside," Tess suggested when they had replaced the rabbits' bedding with fresh, fragrant hay. "I bet they'd like that."

Abby remembered Auntie Jo's rule about house rabbits being outside. "Okay," she agreed. "But we have to supervise them."

Abby carefully picked up Binky, who was heavier, and Tess picked up Marbles. Holding the rabbits firmly against their chests, they carried them into the backyard. The rabbit run was a long, rectangular area enclosed by wire. At one end was a gate with a latch.

Abby opened the gate with one hand and gently set Binky inside. Then she moved aside so Tess could do the same. With both rabbits safely in their run, Abby shut and latched the gate.

"Look," giggled Tess. "They like it out here!"

Binky did one of his famous binkies. He darted down the length of the run, then hopped and twisted in the air, bounding away again as soon as his feet hit the ground. Marbles hopped into a patch of green grass and began nibbling.

"Why can't they live out here all the time?" asked Tess. "My friend at school has a pet rabbit and it lives outside."

"Does she play with it every day?" asked Abby.

Tess shrugged.

"Rabbits need lots of attention and love," Abby told her. "And room to run and play."

"Just like babies," Tess said.

Abby thought about that. "Yeah, that's right. You wouldn't leave Seth and Ian in their crib all day long, would you?"

Tess shook her head vigorously. "No way."

"If you love something, you take care of it,"

Abby said, watching Binky chase Marbles through some dandelions. "Not just physically, but emotionally too. Rabbits get sad and lonely just like people."

An hour passed, and it was time to bring the rabbits back inside the house. Marbles was easy to catch, but Binky led them on a chase. Finally Abby cornered him and scooped him up. They put the rabbits back in the playroom, where they immediately curled up together in the cardboard castle.

Abby walked Tess home, then headed to the Rescue Center to volunteer. Today, however, she made sure she left early. Tess had held up her end of the bargain, and now it was Abby's turn. So at two o'clock she walked back to the apartment and found Tess in the living room, singing to the babies in their infant swings.

"I'm here," Abby announced.

"Woof," barked Tess happily. "Bonding time!"

Tess pushed Ian in his swing and made goofy faces. Ian cooed and waved his chubby arms in the air.

Abby stepped over to Seth's swing. She gave it a gentle nudge and set it in motion. Seth stared at her.

"Try making a face," Tess suggested.

Abby crossed her eyes and put her thumbs in her ears. Seth broke into a wail. "Shhhhhh," said Abby, pushing the swing a tiny bit harder. "Don't cry!"

"Try singing," Tess said over his unhappy cries.

Abby tried singing the monkey song, but she couldn't remember the words. "I'm a little monkey, look at me, something, something, in a tree ..."

Tess snorted. Seth wailed louder.

Desperate, Abby jumped to her feet and flapped her arms. "Ooh, ooh, ahh, ahh," she screeched, doing her best monkey imitation. Seth's wails turned into outright howls. Pretty soon both twins were crying.

"It's not working," Abby panted. Exhausted, she collapsed in a heap on the couch. "They just don't like me."

"Don't give up," Tess pleaded. "Babies cry sometimes. You can't take it so personally."

Abby frowned, recognizing her own words.

"Goodness, what's all the commotion?" asked Mom, stepping into the room. She scooped

Seth out of his swing. "Abby, you're home early today."

"Um, yeah," said Abby, glancing at Tess. "I thought I'd work on my homework." She'd finished her math, spelling, and French, but she still had that essay to write.

"Great, honey," said Mom. She sniffed the air suspiciously, patted Seth's bottom and made a face. "Looks like someone needs a diaper change. Any volunteers?"

"No thanks," said Abby quickly. "I don't think Mr. Laurent wants two thousand words on how I changed diapers over spring break."

CHAPTER 15
Baby Bonding Blues

"Waaaaah!"

Abby groaned and pried open an eye. Her bedside clock said 2:30 am.

"Waaaaah! Waaaaaah!"

She pulled the covers over her head, waiting for Mom or Dad to make it stop.

"WAAAAAAAAAAAAAAH!"

Abby couldn't stand it anymore. She stumbled out of bed and down the hall to the nursery. Seth lay in his crib, his face red from crying.

"What's wrong?" she asked hoarsely. "It's the middle of the night!"

Seth wailed, his cheeks shiny with tears.

Abby glanced at his diaper. No way was she doing diaper duty! She held her breath and checked, but thankfully it was dry.

"Mom already fed you," Abby told him. "And you're not wet. So what's wrong?" Ian, lying in his crib against the other wall, began to fuss too.

"Shhhhh," whispered Abby. "You'll wake up your brother. Do you want your mouse?" asked Abby. She turned on the musical toy and the soft notes filled the air.

Seth's little chest heaved with sobs. He looked so small in the crib. So lonely. Suddenly, Abby had a thought. She went to Ian's crib and carefully lifted him up, supporting the back of his neck the way Mom had shown her. He grunted sleepily, his fingers curled into little fists. Abby carried him over to Seth's crib and gently laid him beside his brother.

Miraculously, Seth stopped crying. Abby smiled as Seth's fingers clutched at Ian's sleeper. The twins reminded her of Binky and Marbles, contentedly snuggling up to each other.

"That's better, isn't it?" she whispered tenderly. It made perfect sense. Like the rabbits, the twins needed more than just food and water. They needed each other. They were bonded, just like the rabbits. They'd spent nine months together in Mom's belly, after all.

Abby rubbed Seth's tummy and he gave a little burp.

"What's going on?"

Abby turned and saw Tess in the doorway, her hands on her hips. For a minute Abby had a vision of

Tess going into guard dog mode and chasing her out of the nursery, growling and snapping. Quickly, Abby put her finger to her lips and pointed at the crib.

Tess looked at the twins, curled together in the middle of the crib. She smiled and hugged Abby. "You're the best big sister ever."

Abby knew that wasn't exactly true. But she decided to try harder. They waited while Seth's eye's closed and his breathing grew even. Then Abby carefully tucked Ian safely back into his own crib and she and Tess tiptoed to their room.

"'Night, Tess," Abby whispered.

Tess's soft snore floated over the wall of diaper boxes. Abby closed her eyes and before she knew it, sunlight was streaming through her window.

Abby groaned and looked at her bedside clock again. 10:30.

She had overslept!

She tugged on her clothes and peeked around the diaper wall. Tess's bed was unmade and empty. She snatched a pair of socks out of her dresser and tried to pull them on as she ran down the hall. It was the last day of pet-sitting, and she was late. What if Auntie Jo returned from her trip and found the rabbits hungry and their cage dirty? What kind of pet-sitter would she think Abby was?

Mom sat at the table, sipping a cup of herbal tea. "Good morning."

"Where's Tess?" Abby asked. "We're late."

"She's in the living room, entertaining the twins." Mom set her teacup down. "She told me that you got up with the twins last night."

Abby shrugged. "It wasn't a big deal."

Mom smiled. "It's a big deal to me. That was the best night's sleep I've had in a long time. I think I might actually have enough energy to make Easter dinner tonight. Thank you, honey."

Abby blushed. "See you later." She grabbed a banana and ran into the living room. The noise was like a slap in the face. Cartoons blared from the television and Tess was singing and bouncing on the couch with a monkey puppet on one hand and a fairy princess puppet on the other.

"I'm going to Auntie Jo's house," Abby shouted.

Tess scratched her head with the fairy puppet. "But I'm in the middle of my show. Seth wants to see how it ends."

Right on cue, Seth began to cry. Tess used the monkey puppet to pick up a plastic tambourine and shook it wildly over her head. She banged on it with the fairy puppet and barked at the top of her lungs. Seth quieted, his eyes following her every move.

"I don't have time to wait for the show to end," Abby yelled over the awful racket. "I'm already late."

"This is just the first act," protested Tess. She jumped up on the coffee table and did an impromptu tap dancing routine. Her shoes clattered against the wood and Abby covered her hands with her ears. This was too much!

"Why don't you stay here," she told Tess. "I don't mind. Really."

"Yippeee!" cried Tess. She popped a kazoo into her mouth and banged harder on the tambourine. The twins gurgled happily. On her way out the door, Abby spied her essay. Impulsively, she stuffed it into her jacket pocket. Maybe she'd have time to work on it at Auntie Jo's.

She sure wasn't going to get enough peace and quiet to write two thousand words around here!

CHAPTER 16

An Appetite for Disaster

Auntie Jo's silent house was a huge relief after the zoo Abby left behind at the apartment. She could finally hear herself think!

Quickly, she pulled some beet greens, pea pods, and radish tops out of the refrigerator. It didn't take her long to clean and fill the food dishes, empty and rinse the litter box, and put fresh hay in the cage. Soon the chores were done.

"Auntie Jo said she'd be home around now," Abby said, glancing at her watch. Binky nudged her foot with his head. Abby smiled. "I guess we can play while we wait."

Abby sat on the playroom floor and rolled a ball toward Binky. He pushed it with his nose, hopped after it, and pushed it again. Marbles joined in and soon they were playing a game of bunny soccer. The ball rolled into the cardboard castle and the rabbits disappeared after it.

Abby checked her watch again. Maybe she

should work on her essay while she waited. It was due tomorrow, after all. She pulled out the papers and smoothed them on the playroom floor. Two thousand words ... and she didn't even have her title yet.

"*How I Spent my Spring Break,*" Abby said out loud. Boring!

"*How I Took Care of Binky and Marbles,*" she tried again. Better. But they weren't the only rabbits she was taking care of.

"*How I Volunteered at the Rescue Center and Helped Save Lots of Rabbits From Neglect and Abuse,*" Abby said. Way too long, but it gave her the perfect idea.

Abby began to write. She described the rescue center and Cocoa Bean and all the rabbits there. She wrote down what she'd learned from Crystal and what she'd learned from the literature she'd gotten at the center. Her pen scratched across the paper furiously, stopping now and then to cross out a word and put a better one in its place. She filled one page, and then another and another.

Finally, she stopped. She flipped through the pages and smiled. Mr. Laurent was going to love this essay. Three pages, and not one word about dogs! All she had to do was proofread it and copy it out neatly.

"Hello?" called a voice. "Anybody here?"

Abby jumped to her feet. "Coming!" She ran to the front room, where Auntie Jo was setting down her suitcase.

"How did it go?" asked Auntie Jo.

"Great," Abby said truthfully. "How was your trip?"

Auntie Jo slipped out of her shoes and tossed her sweater over the back of a chair. "Wonderful. The university is amazing and they have just the courses I want to take. In fact, I've enrolled in an animal shelter management program for the fall semester."

"Wow," said Abby.

"I'm so excited," Auntie Jo confessed. Her eyes sparkled. "There's so much I have to do before summer. I'll have to live in the city ... which means I'll need to find a place where Binky and Marbles and I will be happy, and put this house up for rent and help find a replacement for my job at the Rescue Center ... oh, the list is endless!"

"You're going to rent out this house?" Abby asked, biting her lip.

"I can't leave it empty," Auntie Jo said. "And I'm not quite ready to sell it, even though it is too big for one person."

"I wish I could rent it," Abby muttered. That dormer bedroom would be all hers. No mess, no clutter. No diaper boxes.

"What did you say?" asked Auntie Jo.

"Nothing," Abby said quickly. "I was just thinking it should be easy to find a family to rent out a nice house like this."

"Well, it has to be the right family," Auntie Jo said. "The trouble is, I don't know a lot of young families."

"Maybe my parents can help," Abby found herself offering. "My dad works at the hospital and knows loads of people."

"Good idea," said Auntie Jo, a pensive look on her face. "Why don't I walk you home and have a chat with your parents?"

"Let me get my homework," Abby said, heading back to the playroom. She slowed down when she got to the door so she wouldn't startle the rabbits. She would just grab her essay and –

It was gone!

Confused, she scanned the room. The pen lay on the floor, untouched, but the essay had vanished. She stepped closer and noticed a flash of white through one of the cardboard castle's windows.

"Oh, no," she said, knowing what she would find when she looked inside the castle. "I was only gone a few minutes ..."

She reached her hand through the window and pulled out her essay.

It was completely shredded.

CHAPTER 17
Binky and Marbles to the Rescue!

"Okay, class, settle down," Mr. Laurent said. "We have one last essay to listen to."

The class grumbled, then fell quiet. It was the end of the first day back at school and everyone was ready to go home. Abby stood up and walked to the front of the room. Her hands were empty and she cleared her throat nervously.

"Nice shirt!" Dirk called out. Abby looked down at her "Proud Big Sister" shirt. She had worn it today, hoping it would be lucky.

"My essay is called, "How I saved the Easter Bunny," she began.

"Is your essay invisible?" asked Zach. The class tittered.

"That's enough, boys," Mr. Laurent warned.

Abby stood straighter. She hoped this was going to work. "The truth is, I did write the essay, but then the Easter Bunny ate it."

Dirk snickered. "Yeah, right."

"Actually, two Easter bunnies," Abby continued. She glanced at Mr. Laurent, who was watching her closely. "So I'm doing things a little differently today."

Taking a deep breath, she launched into her speech. "Sometimes at Easter people like to give cute little baby bunnies as gifts. But did you know that thousands of pet rabbits are abandoned every single year? So where do these rabbits end up? If they are lucky, they end up at a place like the Rabbit Rescue Center, where I volunteered over the spring break."

The class was quiet and Mr. Laurent smiled encouragingly. Abby walked to the door and opened it. Auntie Jo stepped inside, carrying a large plastic animal carrier. She nodded at Abby. Abby nodded back, grateful Auntie Jo had agreed to her plan.

"I'd like you to meet Binky and Marbles," said Abby. "And their owner, Josephine Peebles, who works at the Rabbit Rescue Center."

There were oooh's and aaah's from the kids. Everyone strained forward to catch a glimpse of the rabbits. Auntie Jo winked at Dana and Dinah, then carried the rabbits around the classroom so the kids could get a closer look. For the next five minutes Abby talked about everything she'd written in her essay yesterday. She spoke about being a volunteer

at the Rescue Center. She passed around literature and described how she cared for the rabbits. Everyone got a chance to pet Binky and Marbles.

"So remember," Abby said, finishing her talk. "The best kind of Easter Bunny is one made of real chocolate!"

Auntie Jo waved at Abby before she left and Abby sat back down at her desk. Mr. Laurent stood up.

"Thank you, Abby, for that oral report," he said. "It wasn't exactly what I expected, but then again, it didn't have anything to do with dogs. Good job."

Abby breathed a sigh of relief.

When the bell rang, Abby found Tess and they walked home together. Abby tried to open the apartment door, but something was blocking it on the other side. She pushed harder and peeked inside.

"Boxes?" she said, puzzled. She slipped into the apartment sideways and Tess squeezed in behind her. "Mom? What's going on?"

Mom tried to clear a path through several cardboard boxes. "Special delivery for the twins. You know how Gran likes to shop online."

"Did she order the whole store?" asked Abby.

Mom shrugged helplessly. "I think she felt bad

for missing Easter dinner with us this year. There are new car seats and crib bumper pads and bath seats ... everything is times two, of course."

"Of course," Abby said. She sidled toward her bedroom. "Where are we going to put it all?"

"Some of it can be set aside until the twins are bigger," Mom said, looking at a box with a picture of a plastic sandbox on it. "Maybe we could store it in your room, just until – "

"In our room?" Abby stopped, mid-shuffle. "Are you kidding? Our bedroom is crammed full of diapers!"

Tess whimpered.

"Hang on, girls," Mom said. "It's just until – "

"Is Gran crazy?" Abby asked. Her voice rose with every word. "What are we going to do with a sandbox? Set it up under the kitchen table? The apartment just isn't big enough for all this stuff!"

Mom just smiled. "Exactly."

Abby and Tess stared at her.

"You mean ... " whispered Abby.

"Your dad and I were up late last night talking," Mom said. "We know something has to change, but we weren't sure ... and then we talked to your friend Josephine ... we did some calculations and discussed it, and ..."

"We're moving?" Abby hardly dared to breathe.

Mom nodded.

"We're moving!" cried Abby. She grabbed Tess and hugged her until she squirmed. "We're moving, we're moving, we're MOVING!"

"Not until summer," Mom cautioned them. "That's still a few months away ... "

Abby couldn't believe it. "Do you know what this means?" she whispered to Tess.

Tess nodded, her eyes shining.

No more diapers in the bedroom. No more baby swings blocking the computer desk and no more laundry in the bathtub.

And best of all ... maybe not today, maybe not tomorrow, but someday soon ... no more "NO PETS ALLOWED"!

Looking for more pet-sitting fun?

Be sure to check out all the books in the
"ABBY AND TESS PET-SITTERS" series.

Praise for the "Abby and Tess Pet-Sitters" series:

"... likely to tickle the funny bone of a young reader ...
reminiscent of Beverly Cleary's Beezus and Ramona."
– Quill & Quire

"A good read for pet lovers." – School Library Journal

"A really fun combination of weird animals and strong
female characters that deals with the themes of responsibility
and independence." – Kidscreen

"... a mix of animal information, sisterly dynamics,
and a lively plot ..." – Canadian Children's Book News